E
Fuc

Fuchshuber, Annegert
The wishing hat

79-16

DATE DUE			
	10		T-7
	T-20		
FEB 1 2 1990	7		
JAN 3 1 1992	4		
FEB 7 1992	14		
	4		
NOV 9 1995	T 6 / 5		
673160 CL 7/84			

K-3

THE WISHING HAT

written and illustrated

by Annegert Fuchshuber

Translation from the German

by Elizabeth D. Crawford

William Morrow and Company

New York 1977

Library of Congress Cataloging in Publication Data

Fuchshuber, Annegert.
    The wishing hat.

    Translation of Korbinian mit dem Wunschhut.
    SUMMARY: A man acquires a hat that grants his every wish.
    [1. Hats—Fiction.   2. Wishes—Fiction.
3. Magic—Fiction]   I. Title.
PZ7.F94Wi3   [E]   76-54237
ISBN 0-688-22100-9
ISBN 0-688-32100-3 lib. bdg.

One morning Korbinian was very surprised
to find a hat on the table in his apartment
high above the roofs of the big city.

Now who could have forgotten that?
he wondered.

He hadn't had any visitors for a long time—
except Aunt Caroline.
But she never took her hat off.
Besides, this hat was much prettier
than any of the twenty-three lavender hats
Aunt Caroline owned.
And it was yellow, too.
After inspecting it carefully,
Korbinian decided that it must be a wishing hat.

Most people know what to do

with a wishing hat.

But Korbinian had to look it up

in his old book of fairy tales first.

Then he carefully put on the hat,

closed his eyes, turned the hat three times,

the way one is supposed to,

and wished for an apple tree in his living room.

He had dreamed of having one for a long, long time.

Presto!

There was an apple tree,

growing out of the flowered rug.

And it was full of ripe apples.

That afternoon Aunt Caroline came to call.
Of course, she saw the apple tree first thing,
and she was quite upset.
She clapped her hands and cried excitedly,
"Now then, what's all this? What's all this?"

To calm her, Korbinian told her
about his wishing hat.
But he didn't calm Aunt Caroline at all.

"You simpleton!" she scolded.
"You should have wished for a bag of money!"

"I can do that anytime," said Korbinian.

When Korbinian got dressed on Tuesday morning,

he saw to his great annoyance

that his left sock had a hole in it again.

Socks without feet would be much more practical,

he thought.

I have warm slippers anyhow,

and socks without feet

would never have holes in them!

Quickly he put on his wishing hat

and wished for some stockings "up to the knees

and red striped, please, and without feet."

They were on his feet before he had finished speaking.

He hadn't even needed to bend over.

And they pleased him very much indeed.

Right after breakfast Mr. Snodgrass came

to return a book he had borrowed from Korbinian.

In greeting, Korbinian proudly stretched out his feet

to show off his new socks,

but Mr. Snodgrass wasn't very impressed with them.

Perhaps the stripes bothered him,

for he himself always wore gray.

But Korbinian thought

the stripes were just beautiful.

Delightedly he showed Mr. Snodgrass

the apple tree and the wishing hat.

"You simpleton!" said Mr. Snodgrass.

"You should have wished for a big car!"

"I can do that anytime," said Korbinian.

On Wednesday morning Korbinian woke up
with a dreadful stomachache.
It was probably because of the twelve apples
he had eaten for supper on Tuesday.
He put on his hat and wished for a basket
so he could send his cat shopping.
The basket was there
even before Korbinian had taken off
the wishing hat.
There was money in it, too.
Korbinian put a note in it:

1 package of
zwieback
½ pound of
bologna
peppermint tea

And then the cat walked off over the roofs.

That afternoon the grocer came,

panting up the many stairs.

He wanted to know

why Mr. Korbinian hadn't come shopping himself.

Korbinian had taken a big cup

of peppermint tea by that time

and was keeping his stomach warm with the cat

and a thick pillow.

He was feeling much better.

He told the grocer the secret of the basket,

showed him the apple tree,

and stretched out his feet with the new socks.

"You simpleton!" said the grocer, laughing.

"You should have wished for a big house

with a swimming pool!!"

"I can do that anytime," said Korbinian.

On Thursday Korbinian was feeling well again.

As a precaution, though, he ate only zwieback for breakfast.

Then suddenly he felt like going for a walk.

Why else have a wishing hat? he thought,

and he wished for an umbrella

that could fly him to wherever he wanted to go.

But for the first time that week,

nothing happened!

Korbinian put the hat on again

and was just about to repeat his wish

when there came a knock on the door.

He opened it,

and there stood his old black umbrella.

"Aha, so that's it!" said Korbinian.

He opened his umbrella

and wafted through the window with it.

He wasn't dizzy at all,

so he took a nice sightseeing trip

around all the churchtowers of the city.

Korbinian didn't get home from his trip
until late afternoon.
He was so delighted
he did a little dance of pure joy,
and then, one after the other,
he hugged the umbrella, the hat, the cat,
and the apple tree.
Soon the woman from the fifth floor came upstairs.

"What an unbearable racket!" she complained.

Korbinian apologized politely
and showed her the basket, the socks,
the umbrella, the apple tree, and the hat.
But the woman from the fifth floor
wasn't at all sympathetic.

"You simpleton!" she shouted.
"You would have done better to wish
for a modern kitchen!"

"I can do that anytime," said Korbinian.

CAREFUL!
FRESHLY
WAXED!

Because Korbinian was in such a good mood
on Friday morning,
he wished for a flute.
He couldn't play at all,
but he thought that the wishing hat
could probably give him
a flute that would also teach him to play.

The flute was really very patient
and practiced with Korbinian,
first A and then C.
Soon he could play "cuckoo."
He was very happy.

That evening Aunt Caroline paid another visit.

She brought two friends with her this time

to show them the un-be-*liev*-able apple tree.

Korbinian made coffee

and then a little hesitantly

brought out his treasures:

the socks, the basket, the umbrella,

the flute, and the hat.

But he couldn't make any impression with them.

"You simpleton!" jeered the three friends together.

"You should have wished for a chest of jewels

and a fur coat!"

"I can do that anytime," said Korbinian.

The three old ladies each grabbed an apple
and left.

Korbinian was very angry.

He put on his wishing hat,
turned it around three times
the way one is supposed to do,
and wished that the stairs to his apartment
would turn upside down.
Immediately they turned themselves over,
and from above they looked very nice.
Satisfied, Korbinian went back into his apartment.

He sat contentedly in his armchair
under the apple tree, the cat on his lap.

"Now I really have everything I need," he said.
And he threw the hat out the window.

About the Author

Annegert Fuchshuber was born and educated in Germany. For several years she worked as a graphic designer for an advertising agency in Munich. Since 1966, she has devoted herself to book illustration, and she has written and illustrated several books for children.

Mrs. Fuchshuber lives with her husband and three children in Augsburg, Germany.